Duck
in trouble

Jenny Tyler and Philip Hawthorn
Illustrated by Stephen Cartwright

Consultant: Betty Root
Edited by Heather Amery

Here's Duck, who hopes that very soon,
He'll have a big, fat, round balloon.

He starts to rise and holds on tight,
He looks just like a funny kite.

Atchoo! He sneezes, what a shame!
And falls back down to earth again.

He gives poor Bird a dreadful shock,
The nest begins to roll and rock.

The tree branch breaks and with a crack,
They both fall down and Duck says, "Quack!"

Where Duck before was green and scruffy,
Now he looks all clean and fluffy.

So Duck drips dry, but trouble's brewing,
Watch that cat, what is she doing?

As Duck goes splat, he hears a laugh,
Says Cat, "Enjoy your muddy bath!"

Now Duck needs scrubbing, at the double!
Looks like he's in bubble trouble.

The soggy Duck now needs to dry,
He shakes his feathers with a sigh.

Duck goes to bed, he's tired out.
What do you think he dreams about?